Annabelle Swift, Kindergartner

Story and Pictures by
AMY SCHWARTZ

ORCHARD BOOKS

New York

Acknowledgment

Annabelle Swift had her beginnings in a character created by my
older sister, Joan Schwartz, when she was in seventh grade. Joan's
story was published in the San Diego City Schools' creative writing
magazine. Her tale of a spirited youngster, "Jeremy Swift, Kindergartner," impressed me greatly as a first grader, and twenty-six
years later, became the starting point for this book.　　　—A.S.

Orchard Books, 95 Madison Avenue, New York, NY 10016

Manufactured in the United States of America.　10　9　8
The text of this book is set in 14 pt. Meridien. The illustrations are pen-and-ink with
watercolor wash and pencil, reproduced in full color.

Library of Congress Cataloging-in-Publication Data
Schwartz, Amy. Annabelle Swift, kindergartner.
Summary: Although some of the things her older sister taught her at home seem a little unusual at
school, other lessons help make Annabelle's first day in kindergarten a success.　[1. Kindergarten—
Fiction. 2. Schools—Fiction 3. Sisters—Fiction] I. Title PZ7.S406An 1988 [E] 87-15403
ISBN 0-531-07027-1 (pbk.)

For Lenny

Lucy taped the name tag onto her little sister's blouse.

"Annabelle Swift, Kindergartner!" she read. "I remember my first day of kindergarten, Annabelle," Lucy said importantly. "I didn't have a big sister to train me."

Annabelle straightened her name tag.

"I'm going to teach you the fancy stuff, Annabelle. Tomorrow they'll know you're *my* sister."

Annabelle followed Lucy into the den.

Lucy stood by the globe.

"This is the world, Annabelle. *This* is geography."

She peered at the globe and put her finger on a certain spot.

"And this is *us*. Got that?"

Annabelle nodded.

"Good! On to colors!"

Next they went to their mother's dressing table. Lucy coated her lips with lipstick.

"What color's this, Annabelle?"

"Red!"

"*This* is not red," Lucy replied. She read the lipstick label. "This is Raving Scarlet."

She smeared powder under her eyebrows. "And *this* is Blue Desire. Now that you've gotten that, we'll do arithmetic before dinner."

Lucy emptied their father's change dish onto the rug.

"Remember to ask lots of questions, Annabelle. Teachers like that.
Are there numbers less than zero? And what's the number after infinity,
anyway?"

Annabelle didn't answer. She was already counting the pennies
on the rug. Annabelle loved to count.

Lucy had already taught her the numbers past 100.

Annabelle came to a nickel. Lucy had taught Annabelle about nickels. "Remember, a nickel's worth five pennies," Lucy said. She picked up a penny. "One," she counted. Then she took Annabelle's nickel. "Two, three, four, five, six. A nickel and a penny. Six cents."

"Annabelle, call your sister to dinner," their mother called from the kitchen.

Annabelle stood up. She cleared her throat and moved close to Lucy. "Dinner!" she shouted.

Annabelle woke up early the next morning. She practiced counting the nickels and pennies in her father's change dish until her mother told her it was time to get ready. Annabelle ate breakfast and put on the red dress she'd helped pick out for her first day of kindergarten.

Lucy helped Annabelle on with her sweater. "Remember your milk money." Lucy gave Annabelle the nickel and the penny that were lying on the dresser. "And don't forget your name tag. It'll bring you luck."

Annabelle smiled. She put the name tag in her pocket and rubbed it with her finger.

The girls' mother walked with them to school. They dropped Lucy off at
her third grade classroom.

"Good luck, honey," her mother said. "Let the teacher know who's boss."

Lucy hugged her mother. She turned to her little sister and shook her
hand. "Annabelle, remember, you're my sister!"

Annabelle and her mother walked past the second grade room, past the
first grade room, and up to the kindergarten. A tall man opened the door.

"Hello, there. I'm Mr. Blum, the kindergarten teacher."

"Annabelle, Mr. Blum will look after you." Annabelle's mother kissed her
good-bye. "I'll be back at noon to pick you up."

Mr. Blum took Annabelle's hand. "Come join your classmates on the green rug. I'm just calling roll. Watch the other children and you'll know what to do."

Annabelle sat down like the other kids and folded her hands.

"Max Adams?" Mr. Blum called.

A red-haired boy waved his hand.

"Welcome, Max. Edie Cramer?"

"Here!" said a little girl.

Annabelle folded and refolded her hands. Her mouth was dry.
"Lucy," she whispered. "What do I do?" Then she saw the corner of
her name tag sticking out of her pocket and remembered. "My sister told
me how to do this," she said to the chubby boy sitting next to her.

"Annabelle Swift?" Mr. Blum called.

Annabelle jumped up. She cleared her throat.

"Annabelle Swift, Kindergartner!"

All the kids on the green rug started laughing. Except the chubby boy.

Annabelle sat down. She wanted to crawl under the rug.

"Now let's go to the concept corner for the colored lollipop
game," Mr. Blum said. He pulled a construction paper
lollipop out of a box.

"Who knows what color this is?"

"Raving Scarlet," Annabelle whispered to the chubby boy.

"Red!" Edie Cramer called out.

"That's right, Edie," said Mr. Blum.

Annabelle rubbed her name tag with her finger. She counted the buttons on Mr. Blum's shirt.

Mr. Blum pulled out another lollipop. "And this one?"

Annabelle jumped to her feet. "Blue Desire!" she shouted.

Mr. Blum cleared his throat. "It's light blue, Annabelle."

Annabelle sat down. "Drat that Lucy," she whispered to herself.

During recess Annabelle and the chubby boy dragged sticks along the fence.

"Annabelle!" a bush outside the fence said.

Annabelle jumped. Then she recognized the voice.

"Don't worry," she said to the chubby boy. "It's just my sister."

"How's kindergarten?" the bush asked. "Isn't my training a big help?"

Annabelle glared at the bush. "Not exactly," she said. Annabelle dropped her stick. Her lower lip quivered. "Everything I say is wrong."

"Oh, Annabelle," the bush said. "Don't cry. Remember, Annabelle, you're not just any kid. You're Annabelle Swift, Kindergartner!"

The bell rang. Recess was over.

"Put on your name tag," the bush whispered. "It'll help."

The chubby boy helped Annabelle stick on her name tag as they walked inside.

All the kids sat down again on the green rug. Mr. Blum said, "Now we'll have arithmetic. Any questions before we begin?"

Annabelle decided *not* to ask about zero, or infinity.

Mr. Blum pointed to some big numbers on a felt board. "We'll practice counting together first."

The class counted to ten. To herself, Annabelle counted past 100.

"And now . . . snacktime!" Mr. Blum announced. "I'd like all of you to take out your milk money and put it in the middle of the rug."

Everyone piled nickels and pennies on the rug.

Mr. Blum picked up some coins. "A nickel is five cents and a penny is one," he said. "During the year, we'll study nickels and pennies. In June, whoever can count all the money will get to be Milk Monitor. For now, I'll add up the coins myself."

But many of the kindergartners decided to start counting
the milk money right away. Most kids didn't get past ten cents.
Max Adams ran out of fingers. Edie Cramer got the nickels mixed up
with the pennies.

Soon Annabelle was the only kindergartner counting.

"One hundred and five," Annabelle said. "One hundred and six . . . one hundred and seven . . . one . . . hundred . . . and . . . eight!"

The class was stunned.

"Annabelle!" Mr. Blum exclaimed. "That's wonderful! In all my years of teaching, I've never seen a kindergartner count all the milk money on the very first day!"

He shook Annabelle's hand.

"Class, today Annabelle will take the milk money to the cafeteria."

The chubby boy cheered, "Hooray for Annabelle!"

Mr. Blum put all the nickels and pennies in a big yellow envelope. He wrote "$1.08" on the corner and handed it to Annabelle.

"That big pink building at the end of the walkway is the cafeteria," he said. "I'll watch from the window to make sure you get there. Just give the envelope to one of the cafeteria ladies inside."

Annabelle took the envelope. She opened the door and headed for the cafeteria. She walked past the first grade room, and the second grade room.

Clearing her throat rather loudly, she walked past her sister's third grade.

She opened the door to the cafeteria.

"Why, thank you, dear," a big lady wearing a scary red hairnet said.
She took the envelope and handed Annabelle a tray holding eighteen little
cartons of milk and eighteen straws.

Annabelle carried the tray to the cafeteria door.

"Honey, I need to mark down the Milk Monitor for our records," the hairnet lady called after her. "What's your name, dear?"

"My name's Annabelle," Annabelle said.
She slowly opened the door.
Then she carefully turned around, balancing the big tray.
"My name's Annabelle," she repeated. "Annabelle Swift, Kindergartner!"

Then past the third grade room, past the second grade, and past the first, Annabelle Swift, Kindergartner, proudly walked back to rejoin her class.